First published in the United States and Canada in 2015 by NorthSouth Books Inc.,
an imprint of NordSüd Verlag AG, CH-8005, Zürich, Switzerland.

Distributed in the United States by NorthSouth Books Inc., New York 10016.
Library of Congress Cataloging-in-Publication Data is available.

ISBN: 978-0-7358-4215-1
Printed in Latvia by Livonia Print, Riga, May 2015.

3 5 7 9 • 10 8 6 4 2
www.northsouth.com

FSC
www.fsc.org
MIX
Paper from
responsible sources
FSC® C002795

The Adventures of Pettson and Findus
The Fox Chase

Sven Nordqvist

North South

Old man Pettson and his cat, Findus, lived on a little farm out in the country. They had chickens and plenty of firewood, and everything else they needed was in the toolshed. They didn't get many visitors, and that was just as well, thought Pettson.

One day their neighbor Gustavsson, came by with a grim look on his face.

"Hi there, Pettson," he said. "Did the fox pay you a visit, too?"

"No, I haven't noticed a fox here," Pettson said.

"I'm sure you would have noticed if he were," Gustavsson muttered.
"He's a chicken thief. Next time I see him, I'm going to get rid of him."

Then Gustavsson left.

"Well, I suppose we should lock up the chickens in case the fox comes. Right, Findus?"

"I think you should lock up Gustavsson instead," Findus said, staring after him. "I don't trust grumpy old men an inch."

Pettson laughed.

"You don't think he should get rid of the fox?" Pettson asked. "If he doesn't, the fox might eat our chickens."

"You should trick foxes," said Findus. "That's what I always do."

"Yeah, I bet you do." Pettson chuckled. "I agree with you, Findus. We should figure out some way to scare the fox away instead so he'll never want to eat another chicken."

Pettson started thinking. He made sounds when he had a good idea or when he realized his idea wasn't that good. Suddenly he bit at the air and growled, then cackled quietly and said, "Findus, do we have any pepper at home?"

"We always have pepper around," Findus said.

"Then let's go build ourselves a chicken," said Pettson. "You'd better come to the toolshed with me so the fox doesn't get you."

"Pshaw, just let him try," said Findus, but he went along anyway.

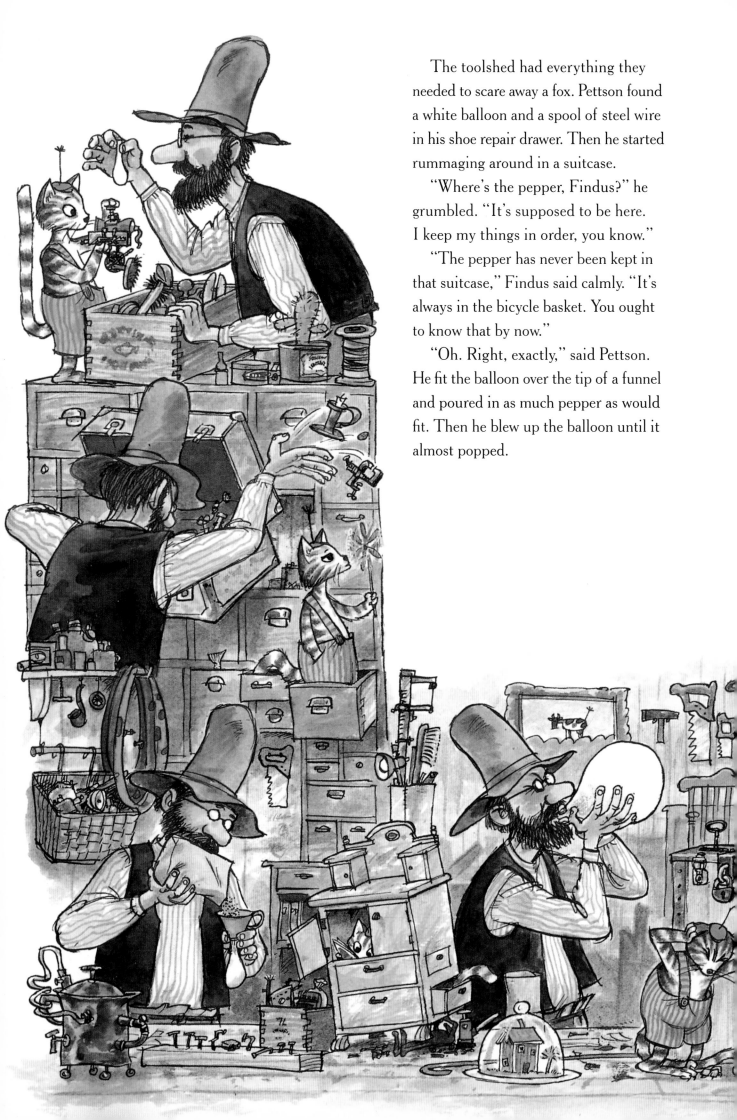

The toolshed had everything they needed to scare away a fox. Pettson found a white balloon and a spool of steel wire in his shoe repair drawer. Then he started rummaging around in a suitcase.

"Where's the pepper, Findus?" he grumbled. "It's supposed to be here. I keep my things in order, you know."

"The pepper has never been kept in that suitcase," Findus said calmly. "It's always in the bicycle basket. You ought to know that by now."

"Oh. Right, exactly," said Pettson. He fit the balloon over the tip of a funnel and poured in as much pepper as would fit. Then he blew up the balloon until it almost popped.

"Now we need some feathers. Do you have any feathers, Findus?"

"I most certainly do not have any feathers," said the cat. "Go ask Giddy."

Giddy was the head hen. She was keeping an eye on what the old man and the cat were up to.

"Giddy! We need some feathers to scare away the fox. You should each give us a few, for your own sakes."

Giddy pursed her beak and went in to see the other chickens. While they clucked and dithered, Pettson wound some wire around the balloon and then shaped it to give it a neck and legs.

Eventually Giddy returned with a bag of feathers.

"We need them back when you're done," she said firmly.

When they were finally finished, the balloon looked almost exactly like a chicken.

"Nice-looking chicken," Findus said. "What are we going to do with it?"

"The fox is going to bite it," Pettson said cheerfully. "He'll come sneaking around at night . . . then he'll spot the chicken and sink his teeth into it: *'Rahhh!'* And then it will explode: *BANG!* And then the fox will be so scared, he'll take a big gasp: *'Aah!'* And then he'll get pepper in his mouth and nose and start sneezing and spitting. And then he'll never eat another chicken again."

The chickens applauded, and Findus looked at the old man with pride.

"You're clever, Pettson," he said.

They put the chicken out in the yard and stood back to admire it.

"It looks great," Findus said.

"Mmm-hmm," Pettson said proudly.

Then they were quiet for a moment.

"I wonder if it's enough though," Findus said. "Shouldn't we add a few more *bang*s while we're at it? So he really gets the message he isn't welcome."

"You like things that go *bang*, huh?" Pettson asked, peering at the cat.

"I'm thinking about the poor chickens," the cat said coolly.

"Of course you're thinking about them," Pettson said. He tugged on his nose and thought for a bit.

"You might be right. We could always set out a few firecrackers, too. You'd better come along so the chicken doesn't explode on you."

"Pshaw, I'm not a fox," Findus said, but he went along anyway.

Pettson went back into the toolshed and started looking in all the old paint cans.
"Where are the firecrackers, if I might ask?" he said, glaring at Findus.
"As far as I know," Findus replied patiently, "they're always in the hatbox by the door."
"Yes, maybe so. Hmm, that's right," Pettson mumbled, stuffing his pockets full of firecrackers and fuse cord and bottle rockets from the hatbox.

They went outside and arranged the firecrackers all around the yard, then Pettson routed the fuse cord inside and over to his bed. Then he placed a box of matches next to it.

"There. That ought to be enough to scare a fox," he said. "When the fox comes tonight, he'll pounce on the balloon chicken and bite into it so it pops. Then when we hear the *bang*, I'll light the fuse, and a second later the whole yard will start banging and flashing. If THAT doesn't scare him, I don't know what kind of a fox he is."

Findus stood by quietly, eyeing the fuse. Then he said, "Foxes are actually pretty stupid. I wonder if a few firecrackers are really going to be enough to convince him not to steal chickens. Couldn't we haunt him a little while we're at it?"

"Hmm, you and your scare schemes!" the old man grunted. "I think this is plenty."

But as Pettson said that he started thinking about how one might go about arranging a good scare, and the more he thought about it the funnier it became. Soon he was standing out in the yard again muttering.

Finally he said, "We'll build a zip line. You'd better come along, Findus, so nothing blows up under your tail."

"Pshaw, the things you say!" Findus said, but he went along anyway.

Pettson stared at the wall inside the toolshed and said, "I used to have a long rope. I hung it on that nail. Now there's a violin hanging there! Are you playing some kind of trick on me, Findus?"

Findus groaned and replied, "You never hung any rope on that nail, Pettson. You put it in the tire."

"Huh, I guess so," the old man mumbled, taking the rope out of the tire. Then he found a sheet and a wheel attached to an iron bar.

He went outside and strung the rope from the roof of the house to the tree on the far side of the front yard. Then he hung the wheel from the rope.

"Come and take a ride on the zip line, Findus," he said.

The cat climbed up the ladder, and Pettson draped the sheet over him and showed him how to hold on. Then he gave him a push.

"YIPPPPEEEEEE!" The cat ghost flew across the yard and a few seconds later hopped off into the tree on the far side.

"Yes, that'll work," said Pettson. "So tonight when I light the fuse, you run up to the attic and put on the sheet, and then when all the banging and flashing is at its peak, you hop out the window, grab on to the zip line, and when you're directly over the fox, you yell as frighteningly as you can: 'DON'T STEAL CHICKENS!' He ought to get the message then."

"Yes, you'd think so," Findus said. He was satisfied now that there would be fireworks, a ghost, and a zip line.

"That ought to do it," Pettson said. "Let's go in and have some coffee."

And so they did.

It was an exciting evening. Before it got dark, Pettson brought all the chickens inside, into the kitchen. He told them they had to be quiet and that if they saw the fox, they should run and wake Pettson up.

After they went to bed, they ran through what was
going to happen one more time: In the middle of the
night, the fox would come, pop the balloon chicken
that would wake them up, Pettson would light
the fuse, and Findus would run up to the attic.
When the firecrackers out in the yard were
at their loudest, Findus would jump onto
the zip line and slide down screaming,
"DON'T STEAL CHICKENS!"
And then the fox would leave and
never come back.

   "That's what's going to
happen tonight," they thought.
In a few hours . . . or a few
minutes . . . or in
the next second . . .

Findus was so tired from being nervous that he fell asleep. But Pettson just lay there, listening. Everything was quiet.

No, it wasn't! He heard something. Or did he just sense that there was something out there in the dark?

Pettson slipped out of bed and peeked out the window. There was the fox! He was sneaking around the chicken coop, sniffing. He looked scared, a poor, skinny little thing with a limp in one of his hind paws.

"Maybe that's why he's been stealing chickens," Pettson thought. "He probably isn't able to catch a hare. He'll have a heart attack if we set off the fireworks. I'm not going to light the fuse."

The fox spotted the balloon chicken standing alone in the middle of the yard. He rushed forward but suddenly stopped right in front of it. He sniffed it cautiously and then ran off, disappearing behind the house.

Pettson watched the fox jump over the fence and sit down, watching the house. The old man felt sorry for him. "It's terrible that Gustavsson was going to get rid of him," he thought.

The clock on the wall ticked slowly. Everything was quiet and still.

Then came a *BANG!* The chicken balloon exploded! Someone started sneezing and spitting loudly.

Findus flew up from the bed as if he were on a trampoline and screamed, "LIGHT THE FUSE, PETTSON!" When he saw that the old man wasn't there, he lit it himself, and two seconds later the whole yard started popping and banging and flashing.

Findus raced up to the attic, pulled on the sheet, opened the window, flung himself onto the zip line, and screamed, "DON'T HUNT FOXES!"

Huh? That's not what he was
supposed to say. He said the
wrong thing.
But actually it was right. Because
just as he finished screaming, he saw that
it wasn't the fox standing in the middle
of the hullabaloo. It was Gustavsson
and his dog! The dog was howling, and
Gustavsson was staring at the ghost
swooping toward him. He squeaked
in a pitiful voice, "Help! I promise
I'll never hunt another fox.
Stop! Let me go!"

And then suddenly it was quiet. The bottle rockets were done, and the cat ghost had disappeared up into the tree. The dog had run away, and Gustavsson just stood there, totally confused, looking around.

One lone firecracker, which hadn't gone off properly, started fizzing.

"Ack!" Gustavsson shuddered and ran away up the road.

When everything was calm and quiet, Findus hopped down from the tree and ran into the kitchen. Pettson was sitting there laughing.

"You did great, Findus," he said. "It didn't turn out how we imagined, but that fox definitely won't be coming back here."

"What do you mean? The fox wasn't here; Gustavsson was," Findus said, looking totally disappointed.

"The fox was here, too," said Pettson. "He didn't want the balloon chicken, but he saw it explode, and the fireworks, too. He was so scared, he came right into the kitchen and was surrounded by ten chickens—staring at him. He turned right around again. He probably thought they were going to explode, too. Although he did manage to grab the chocolate pudding we were going to have for dessert tomorrow."

"That sneaky fox," Findus said. "But . . . we can let him have that. You'll make more chocolate pudding for us, right, Pettson?"

"Yes, of course." Pettson was happy to do that.

Make a Chicken Piñata

Please note: This project requires help from an adult!

Materials:

A balloon
Old newspapers
Plain flour and water
String
Craft scissors

White paint
Yellow tissue paper
Glue
Googly eyes
Assorted candy

Simple steps:

- Blow up a balloon and ask an adult to tie a knot in it.
- Tear the newspaper into strips about 1 inch wide and 6 inches long.
- Mix flour with water so that it's a runny paste.
- Carefully dip each newspaper strip into the paste. Rub your fingers over it to wring out the excess water. Then lay each strip on the balloon so that it is completely covered (except for a 1-inch area around the balloon tie). Add 4 layers of newspaper strips to the balloon to make it sturdy.
- Tie some string to the balloon tie and hang the balloon outside in the sun or a warm part of the house. It may take 2 days to dry thoroughly.

Add the finishing touches:

- Once the strips are thoroughly dry, ask an adult to cut a hole in the top of the balloon (around the tie) so candy can be added later.
- Paint the balloon white. Let the paint dry.
- Add tissue paper "feathers." You can cut the yellow tissue paper into rectangles (1 inch by 2 inches) by folding over a few sheets of tissue and cutting the rectangles to make feathers.
- Glue the feathers on by putting a spot of glue on just one end so that the other end can flutter.
- Glue on the googly eyes.
- Add the candy to the chicken.
- Ask an adult to make 2 small holes at the top of the piñata, then string the twine into the holes and hang your piñata. Enjoy!

Be sure to check out the first three books in the series!

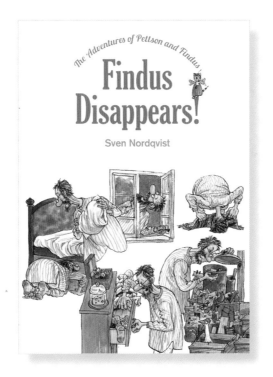

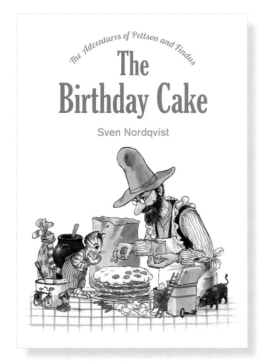